SHAMPOOZEL

Written by Laurence Anholt
Illustrated by Arthur Robins

ORCHARD BOOKS
338 Euston Road,
London NW1 3BH
Orchard Books Australia
Hachette Children's Books
Level 17/207 Kent Street, Sydney, NSW 2000
First published in Great Britain in 1999. This edition published in 2002.
Text © Laurence Anholt 1999. Illustrations © Arthur Robins 1999.
The rights of Laurence Anholt to be identified as the author
and Arthur Robins as the illustrator of this work
have been asserted by them in accordance with the
Copyright, Designs and Patents Act, 1988.
A CIP catalogue record for this book is available from the British Library.
ISBN 978 1 84121 392 7
8
Printed in Great Britain

ORCH/

☆ Ghostyshocks ☆ Snow White ☆ Cinderboy ☆ Eco-Wolf ☆
☆ The Greedy Farmer ☆ Billy Beast ☆

There was once a jolly hairdresser named
Dan Druff.

Dan LOVED hair!

Curly hair and bristly hair, eyebrows and beards – Dan loved them all. He loved the gleam of his many mirrors and the snippety-snick of sparkling silver scissors.

Dan even sang about hair.

Only one thing upset Dan's happiness –
his girlfriend, Tam O'Tei, who lived in
the flat upstairs.

Unlike Dan, Tam was a sad person who hid away in her bedroom behind tightly drawn curtains. From under their hairdryers, Dan's customers could hear her wretched moans and Dan nearly tore his hair out with worry over her condition.

The awful truth was...

...Tam O'Tei had terrible hair!

"Oh, Dan," she wailed. "My head is dull and lifeless. I have a flaky scalp and unsightly split ends, but no ordinary shampoo is effective."

Dan could find nothing to help, and as the days passed, Tam's hair grew as greasy as a chip-shop mop.

Now, not far from the barber shop was an evil black tower which twisted into the sky like a strange hairstyle.

This was the home of the Bad Hair Witch.

High in her dark rooms, the Bad Hair Witch mixed strange shampoos and hair-oils which were sold all over the world. The secret ingredients came from rare plants which grew only in her private garden.

Above the barber shop, Tam became convinced that one of these magical hair herbs would bring life back to her dull scalp and she pleaded with Dan to pick some.

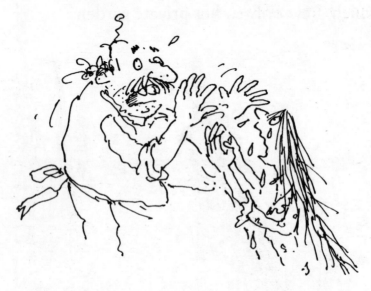

At the mention of the black tower, Dan Druff felt the hairs prickle at the back of his neck.

"I dare not go there," he whispered. "What if I should fall into the evil hair-grip of the Bad Hair Witch?"

14

But Tam O'Tei complained so long and hard that at last Dan Druff could stand it no longer. "All right, keep your hair on," he bristled. "I will go to the tower and comb the gardens for your herbs."

15

So the next morning, before dawn, the
brave barber crept reluctantly up the hairpin
bends that led to the tower.

As he walked, he sang to keep up his courage.

Before he could finish his song, Dan had almost walked into a huge sign hanging on the wall before him:

DAN DRUFF
USE YOUR HEAD
IF YOU CLIMB THIS
WALL
YOU'LL WISH YOU
WERE DEAD

Dan felt a shiver run along his moustache.
Only the thought of Tam's sad locks drove
him on. Ignoring the sign, he scrambled
into the Bad Hair Witch's secret garden
where he found a second sign:

DAN DRUFF, CAN'T YOU READ?
DON'T EVEN THINK
ABOUT NICKING A WEED

Poor Dan had never been in such a hairy situation, but he bent down and began to stuff his pockets with the herbs.

Suddenly he heard a terrible voice:

"Dan Druff, you must be crazy,
You'll pay for those plants,
With your very first baby."

Dan's hair stood on end – it was the worst rhyme he had ever heard.

Before him stood…the Bad Hair Witch!

"B-but I don't have a b-baby," stammered
Dan.

"Well, let's not split hairs," snapped the
witch. "I will wait until your first child
is born."

Grabbing a last handful of herbs, Dan leapt over the wall and hared down the hill to the town.

He found Tam in her bedroom wearing a paper bag on her head, and he poured out the story of his terrifying brush with the Bad Hair Witch.

But Tam was barely listening. She seized
the wonderful herbs, crushed them and
began to lather her scalp...

As if by magic, Tam's hair turned into a glorious mass of glossy curls which seemed to flow in slow motion when she tossed her head.

Tam O'Tei was cured!

26

She tore downstairs into the sunny shop, and, as Dan shaved the bristly early morning customers, Tam happily set to work beside him, sweeping up the fallen curls and locks.

That very week, Tam and Dan were married and the whole town joined them in this glorious hymn:

Before a year was out, the couple's happiness was complete – a beautiful baby daughter was born, and, after much thought, they called her…

In that happy hairy world, not one
thought was given to the Bad Hair Witch.

But the Bad Hair Witch had forgotten
nothing.

High in her tower she worked day and night on her most amazing invention yet – something all barbers dream of – a marvellous, magical HAIR GROWING LOTION!

"Guess which witch will be rich?" she sniggered. "All I need is a helpless, hairless baby to test my invention."

And so the Bad Hair Day dawned. The bell at the little barber shop tinkled cruelly as the Bad Hair Witch burst inside.

"Give me the child!" she shrieked.

"Have you got an appointment?" said
Tam. "Let's see, I could fit you
in on Thursday…"

"You don't understand, you fools. I
need to test my new improved formula –
Ultimate 2-in-1 Hair Growing Lotion."

"Leave Shampoozel alone," pleaded Tam O'Tei. "You cannot try out your hair-brained inventions on our child."

Ignoring the tears of the unfortunate couple, the Bad Hair Witch seized Shampoozel and carried her back to the tower.

To make sure the precious child would
never be taken from her, the Hair Witch
bricked up the front door behind them.

As the days passed, the Bad Hair Witch grew to love the baby and looked after her as if she were her own.

She would sing as she washed the infant's hair:

No more tears, Baby Shampoozel,
My magic shampoo is very unusual.

And day by day, as Shampoozel grew, her hair grew too, in great long golden tresses which tumbled across the floor, down the stairs, into the kitchen, under the dog, round the back of the fridge and back upstairs again.

"Hair, hair, HAIR!!" cackled the Bad Hair Witch. "Look at all your beautiful golden hair!"

Sometimes hairy Shampoozel remembered her parents' little barber shop in the town far below.

Now that their daughter had gone, Dan and Tam worked sadly and never sang anymore; and so, one by one, the customers went elsewhere.

Years passed, and as Shampoozel grew into a young woman, the Bad Hair Witch taught her the secret art of the hairdresser:

Wash your hair and keep it sweet.
Lather, rinse, repeat.
Rub and comb and keep it neat.
Lather, rinse, repeat.

Together, the Bad Hair Witch and Shampoozel created new hair products which were more amazing than anyone could have dreamed of.

They became so famous, in fact, that a young prince by the name of Gary Baldie heard about them from his home in a distant land.

The prince, although handsome and wealthy, was as bald as a billiard ball.

Prince Gary had tried one wig-maker after another but without satisfaction so when he finally heard about Ultimate 2-in-1 Hair Growing Lotion, he set out straight away, and after many days arrived at the tower.

Of course even a prince cannot enter a tower without a door. So Prince Gary concealed himself beneath the walls and after a while he saw an amazing thing.

The Bad Hair Witch appeared at the window with her shopping bag. All of a sudden a great mass of hair cascaded to the ground. The witch slid down it and set off towards the town.

"I suppose that's what they call a hair slide!" whispered Prince Gary in amazement.

Half an hour later, the old lady returned
with her shopping and called out:

Shampoozel, Shampoozel,
Let down your hair,
So I can climb to the top
Of your long hairy stair.

Shampoozel let down her locks again
and the old woman scrambled back up
the tower.

Gary Baldie was no fool and the next time the old woman went out, the prince stood below the window himself and called:

Shampoozel, Shampoozel,
Your hair is so curly,
Let it hang down now,
Be a good girlie.

To his delight, a great coil of hair tumbled to the ground. He seized it and began to baldly go where no man had gone before.

The prince scrambled into Shampoozel's room, and when his royal eyes fell on the lovely Shampoozel he was captivated by her hairiness.

He leaned towards her and kissed her ruby red lips.

There and then, Shampoozel and the prince fell in love. Gary told her that he adored her limitless locks, and how he would love to have some of his own.

To his amazement, Shampoozel replied that she had grown tired of her hair. "It don't half hurt when people climb up it," she complained. "And it takes a week to wash."

But then, to the prince's joy, Shampoozel pulled out a tiny bottle of Ultimate 2-in-1 Hair Growing Lotion and began to massage his shiny scalp. Almost immediately, a single hair popped out of the prince's head.

The first hair was followed by a second, the  second by a third, and within ten minutes the prince had a mass of golden curls snaking down his back, nearly as long as Shampoozel's.

53

Gary Baldie seized Shampoozel and danced with joy.

"My prince, you must wash and go," whispered Shampoozel.

She brushed a few stray hairs from his collar, and with one final kiss, the prince climbed down Shampoozel's hair and slipped away into the shadows.

It wasn't long before the Bad Hair Witch returned.

Shampoozel, Shampoozel,
Don't make me shout,
Let down your hair, Girl,
Don't hang about.

As soon as she entered the salon, the witch spotted Gary Baldie's little crown, which Shampoozel had left hanging on the coat hook.

The witch was furious and, after a terrible argument, stormed into her bedroom, leaving Shampoozel weeping pitifully.

The prince, meanwhile, had decided that witch or no witch, he had to see Shampoozel again. He stood at the foot of the tower and whispered:

Shampoozel, Shampoozel,
Here is your prince,
Throw down your pigtail,
My hair needs a rinse.

Immediately, a long lock of hair curled out of the window and tumbled to the ground.

But just as the prince was about climb up, he saw a figure sliding down...

It was Shampoozel!

"I don't know why I didn't think of this before," she said. "All that stupid hair. I snipped it off and tied it to the bed. Then I slid down to you. At last we have escaped from the Bad Hair Witch."

"That was a close shave!" replied Gary Baldie, softly stroking her silky stubble. "Come on, let's really let our hair down."

So Shampoozel and her hairy prince ran away to his castle, but she didn't forget her parents, Dan Druff and Tam O'Tei.

Although they were rich, Shampoozel and
Gary Baldie liked to work in Dan's shop
on Saturdays.

Before long, the little barber-shop was
once again the busiest in the land.

"It's amazing how the customers keep coming back," laughed Dan.

And it was true – some of the customers seemed to have as many as five haircuts a day.

62

Perhaps they just loved having their hair
cut by Shampoozel.

Or perhaps the secret shampoo she uses
has something to do with it...

Or perhaps they come for the endless
happy songs which drift across the
hairy town...

High in her tower, even the Bad Hair
Witch joins in:

Hair, hair, SENSATIONAL hair,
Shampoozel's the girl,
To share your hair care.
She can give you a shave,
Or a permanent wa-a-ve,
Hair, HAIR...
H·A-A-A-A-I-I-I-R-R-R!!!!